The Australian Echidna

Acknowledgements

I wish to thank Dr. M. E. Griffiths, on whose research much of the information in this book is based, and who kindly read the manuscript.

Photo credits

Cover, pages 1, 4, 10 (bottom), 14 (right), 20 (all three), 24, and 25 Kathie Atkinson; pages 6 (bottom), 7, 15, 21 (top), 28, 29 (right), 30 (bottom), 32, and 35 (top) David Parer; pages 8 (bottom), 10 (top), 12, 14 (left), 21 (bottom), 26, 33, 34 (all three), 35 (bottom), 36, 37, and 38 Elizabeth Parer-Cook; page 30 (top) E. Slater; pages 6 (top), and 22 (both) E. Stodart. Courtesy National Photographic Index of Australian Wildlife: page 8 (top) F. Park; pages 9, and 39 C. Henley; page 11 D. Watts; page 16 H. Frauca; page 17 Fr. A. Eames; pages 18 (both), and 19 E. Beaton; page 23 H. and J. Beste; page 29 (left) Qld. Museum.

Library of Congress Cataloging-in-Publication Data

Stodart, Eleanor.
    The Australian echidna/Eleanor Stodart. — 1st American ed.
        p. cm.
    "Originally published in Australia in 1989 by Houghton Mifflin
Australia Pty. Ltd." — T.p. verso.
    Summary: An introduction to the physical characteristics, habits,
and natural environment of the Australian echidna, also called spiny
anteater.
    ISBN 0-395-55992-8
    1. Spiny anteater—Australia. [1. Spiny anteater.
2. Anteaters.] I. Title.
QL737.M73S76 1991
599.1—dc20   90-33538
                                                CIP
                                                AC

Printed in Hong Kong

10 9 8 7 6 5 4 3 2 1

The Australian Echidna

Eleanor Stodart

Houghton Mifflin Company
Boston 1991

Echidnas are spiny and they eat ants, so they are also called spiny anteaters. People sometimes call them porcupines, but true porcupines have gnawing teeth, and do not eat ants or lay eggs; the name 'echidna' is less confusing.

For many thousands of years echidnas were known to Aborigines as part of the life around them. Just two hundred years ago these spiny anteaters were strange and new to Western naturalists, who discovered their existence only when Europeans began to explore and settle the Australian continent.

At first, the more the Western naturalists learned about echidnas the more puzzled they were. Echidnas are warm-blooded, have hair, and produce milk to feed their young, like all mammals, and their skull is similar to the skull of other mammals. Yet they lay eggs with leathery shells, as reptiles do, and parts of their skeleton are more like a reptile's than a mammal's. The Western naturalists had worked out a system for classifying the animals they knew, and echidnas did not quite fit.

Mammals produce milk for their young.
Top: a cow feeds its calf.
Bottom: a grey kangaroo feeds its joey.

A platypus.

The only other hairy, warm-blooded animal in the world that lays eggs and produces milk for its young is the platypus. European naturalists had not seen a platypus, either, till about two hundred years ago, and the platypus caused even more of a sensation than the echidna because as well as being like a reptile and a mammal it also has a bill like a duck's!

As they learned more, the naturalists decided to classify the echidna and the platypus as mammals, not reptiles. They put them together, with the mammals, in a special group called the monotremes. That is, they broadened our ideas about mammals to include these two that lay eggs, even though all other mammals give birth to their young.

A short-beaked echidna of Australia and the New Guinea lowlands.

A long-beaked echidna of the New Guinea highlands.

Two types of echidna live in the world today. Each has a long snout, but one has an even longer snout than the other.

The type with the shorter snout lives in Australia and the lowlands of New Guinea, and is called the short-beaked echidna. The other lives in the highlands of New Guinea, and looks like the Australian one except that it is bigger and has a longer curved snout. It is called the long-beaked echidna, and it eats earthworms and larger insects from leaf litter.

In this book we will be looking at the short-beaked or Australian echidna.

Echidnas, with their long thin snout and small mouth, short stubby legs, and spines all over the back and sides, are not easily mistaken for any other animal. They can be creamy brown or much darker, because the spines vary in color. As you can see in the photograph, each spine has a dark tip and a light band. If there is a lot of black at the tip, the echidna will appear dark, but if the pale band is wide, the echidna will look much paler.

The ants crawling among the spines are meat ants.

When you first look at an echidna you may not think that it has hair, or fur, like other mammals; but it does. The spines themselves are large stiff hairs, like those of hedgehogs and porcupines. More normal hairs also grow between the spines (as the close-up on page 9 shows), and on the face, belly and legs.

The color of these finer hairs varies from animal to animal, as you can see in these and following pictures. The length varies, too. Tasmanian echidnas may have hair so long that it almost hides the spines. Echidnas need more fur in the cold climate of Tasmania to keep themselves warm.

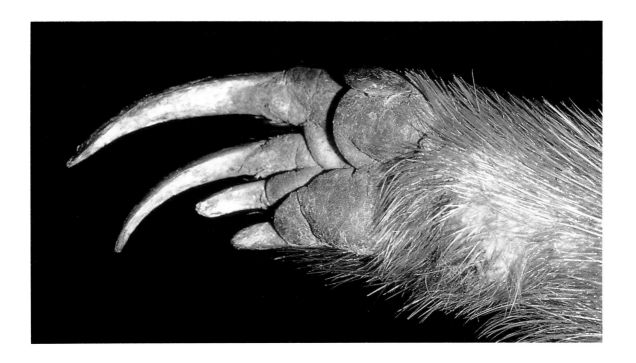

You can imagine that all those spines might make scratching an itch rather awkward, but echidnas have two toes on their hindfeet with extra long claws which can reach down between the spines.

Tasmanian echidna shelters in burrow.

Even despite their fur, echidnas sometimes lower their body temperature in cold weather. They become torpid and hibernate, rather as squirrels and hedgehogs do. In fact they are not very good at keeping their body temperature at a constant level.

In cool weather they burn more fuel; in other words they use more food and oxygen to keep warm, just as people do. But when the weather gets colder still, they stop feeding, go cold, and hibernate. This means that in cool weather they are often active only in the warmer parts of the day; in very cold weather they are less active, or not active at all, and they hide away in a burrow or other shelter.

Echidnas can also have trouble maintaining a constant temperature in very hot weather. They do not sweat, as we do to lose heat from exertion, so in hot weather they manage by being active at night and avoiding the heat of the day. In northwest Western Australia, for instance, they spend the day in small underground caves which stay much cooler than the air above ground.

From the wet east coast . . .

A furry Tasmanian echidna in its cool moist environment.

Echidnas live all over Australia, from the heat of the tropics to the cold of the Snowy Mountains and Tasmania; from the wet east coast to the dry, dry center. That is a wide range of climates and habitats for any one kind of animal to live in, but all these places have one thing in common — ants live there. Spiny anteaters need ants for food. They also eat termites when they are available.

. . . to the dry center.

Even though echidnas occur so widely over Australia, you do not often see them. There are several reasons why. They are well spaced out and live alone, except in the mating season (July and August). They are more likely to be active at night, except when it is cold. And when they do move about by day their coloring camouflages them, and their short legs keep them close to the ground.

When an echidna is disturbed on very hard ground, such as a road surface, it may run away. But if it is disturbed on softer ground it will dig in. As if by magic, it sinks below the ground in an instant. Both

front and back legs quickly dig away the dirt below so that the echidna's whole body sinks down at once. The short stout legs, with their wide flattened feet, five toes on each, make strong and effective shovels. The leg bones are firmly attached to the body skeleton, which means that the legs cannot move freely (as in the way we swing our arms), but they can dig and grip strongly. If you caught up with an echidna before it could bury itself completely, you would find that it was stuck too fast for you to move. Its soft underbelly would be protected and only the spiny back exposed.

The echidna curls into a ball when it is disturbed.

If an echidna is disturbed in a place where it cannot dig in or run away, it will curl up into a ball so that the spines stick out all around and the soft belly is protected in the middle. Even so, at times echidnas fall prey to animals such as dingoes or goannas.

Turned over, all that shows are more spines and a couple of claws.

Now undisturbed for a while, it begins to unroll.

Young echidnas are much easier to catch before the spines are fully grown. This young one was rescued from the goanna shown below.

An ant road leads to a meat ants' nest.

Echidnas dig into meat ant mounds, often making much deeper holes than this.

The echidnas' skill at digging not only protects them from enemies but it also helps them raid ant nests and termite mounds. The common meat ants have very large nests which echidnas attack mainly between August and October, when there are many winged virgin queens with plenty of fat. These queen ants store the fat ready to keep themselves going when they fly away to set up their own nests. When echidnas eat the queens the fat keeps them going instead, but there are still some queen ants left to start new ant nests.

The cloud of dust shows where the echidna is digging, as it tackles the base of a termite mound.

Echidnas raid a variety of other ants at other times, and termite nests as well.

When an echidna digs into a nest it smells out the ants or termites and feels for them with its sensitive snout. It thrusts the snout in and out of the broken nest, flicking out its tongue which is covered in a specially sticky saliva. When a number of ants or termites are stuck to the tongue the echidna pulls it in, dirt and all — for a lot of dirt sticks to the tongue with the ants. Echidnas often eat as much dirt as they eat ants or termites.

Two other special characteristics that echidnas have for living on ants and termites are the small mouth and no teeth. So they cannot chew their food — and they cannot yawn!

Having no teeth to chew with does not mean that echidnas swallow the ants whole. They crush them between the spiny base of the tongue and the roof of the mouth, and the grains of dirt help with the crushing. The crushed ants and dirt are then swallowed down into the stomach. Echidnas and other ant-eating mammals have a stomach with a rather skin-like lining, quite different from the more delicate stomach lining of most mammals.

The long snout, long thin tongue and sticky saliva, small mouth and no teeth, and skin-like lining to the stomach, all make echidnas very specialized for eating ants. It is in the way they produce their young — that is, reproduce themselves — that they seem primitive.

In all but the very simplest animals and plants it is necessary for a male 'seed' (the sperm or pollen grain, or whatever it is called in that particular organism) to join with the female 'seed' (usually called the ovum). Once the two have joined, the now fertilized egg can grow into a new young animal or plant, if given the right conditions. These conditions vary greatly from animal to animal and plant to plant.

Land animals need some method of getting the sperm to the ovum without it drying out and dying. This is usually done by the male mating with the female, and squirting his sperm directly into her vagina where it can swim through her reproductive system to the ovum. The special organ the male uses for this is called the penis. (Many male animals also use their penis for urinating.)

You may have seen a dog mounting a bitch or a bull mounting a cow. This is how the male gets his penis into the female's vagina to place his sperm there. The spiny echidna would find mounting the female rather prickly, but he still needs to insert his penis into her vagina. So they mate lying belly to belly.

The male squirts many hundreds of sperm into the female, and they all swim towards the ovum. Only one joins with the ovum. The egg then has the full number of genes, with half from each parent, and so it can develop.

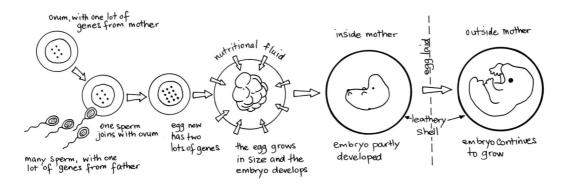

In echidnas the egg first grows in size, fed by nutritional fluid while passing through the uterus. It has a yolk and a layer of albumen (like the white of a hen's egg, but the egg overall does not look like a hen's egg). When at last it is ready to be laid it has a leathery covering but it no longer has a distinct area of yolk, for the young embryo has begun to grow and has already used much of the yolk. In this way echidnas are quite different from the egg-laying birds and reptiles, whose eggs don't begin to develop until after they have been laid.

It takes about three weeks till the egg is ready to be laid. Mating occurs during July and August (that is, in mid to late winter). Three weeks later a shallow pouch forms in the skin of the female's belly, and she lays the egg. Like marsupials (the mammals with a pouch), the echidna has a pouch, although it is there only during breeding.

The female lays the egg directly into her pouch, and hairs hold the egg in place. It is kept warm there, and the embryo continues to grow using the food and fluid in the egg.

A well developed pouch, as it would be when the young is ready to leave it.

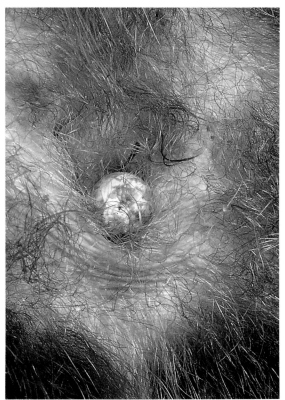

The egg in place in the new pouch.

29

This newborn tammar wallaby looks very similar to the hatching echidna above.

About ten days later the young echidna breaks through the leathery eggshell, using the egg tooth on its snout, and hatches. Apart from having an egg tooth it is surprisingly like a newborn marsupial, as it has a large head, covered eyes, well developed front legs, and tiny back legs.

It is already in the pouch, and it stays there holding on to the hairs with its front legs, for there is no teat for it to grasp in its mouth as the young marsupial does. The mother secretes milk from pores in the skin of her belly. These pores are just like the pores on teats except that they are not raised up on a teat. The young echidna sucks up the milk from the skin and hairs.

The young stays in the pouch, growing steadily, for up to two months. By then its spines have begun to grow, and the mother digs a burrow for it to shelter in. The mother's pouch starts to disappear now because it is no longer used.

*Even when growing spines, the young echidna
fits in the palm of a hand.*

The mother visits the young in the burrow to feed it milk. Her visits are often several days apart, and the young drinks a lot of milk each time. All through its life an echidna can gorge itself on very large meals and then not eat for some time. Echidna milk is richer than human or cow's milk; it has less water and more fat. Babies and calves are fed often, so they do not need such rich milk. The mother echidna rapidly releases plenty of milk so that the young can drink it quickly.

This burrow was made specially for the echidna, to allow for filming. Normally inside the burrow would be quite dark. The mother enters.

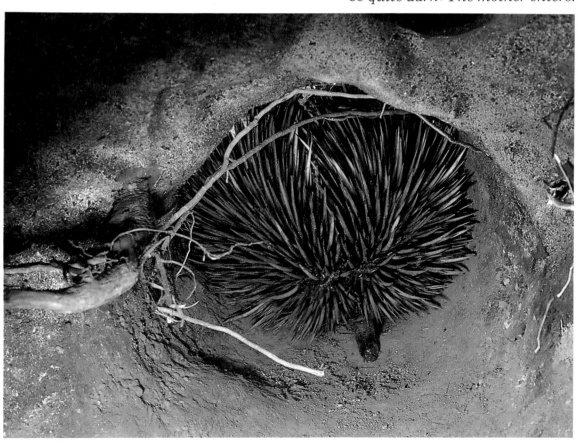

The young struggles up to make its way to its mother, then snuggles underneath for a drink of milk.

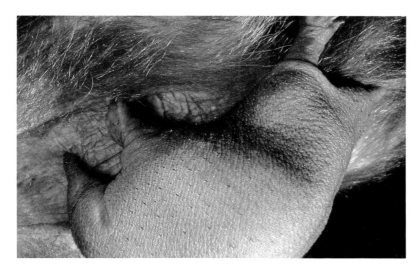

35

At first the spiny young echidna cannot walk well enough to get itself out of the burrow, but its coordination improves and it starts to crawl around. After about five months it is able to walk right out and become independent of the mother. It is then about seven months old.

We don't know just how much effort the mother spends on teaching the young how to find ants and termites for itself. It may know how to find them instinctively, and so may not need any instruction.

As with most animals in the wild, many of the young echidnas end up providing a meal for other animals — perhaps for dingo pups, a goanna mother, or a feral cat. But enough survive to mature and have their own young.

The cycle of life goes on.

GLOSSARY

albumen — the egg white. Provides water and some nutrients for the developing embryo.

embryo — the developing young of a living thing, while still inside the egg, womb of mother, or seed.

feral — feral animals are pets or domestic animals that have gone wild and are no longer cared for by people.

gene — very tiny units within each cell of living things. They determine all the characteristics of the living thing, and are passed on from parent to young so that the young inherit characteristics from the parents.

hibernate — to spend the winter, or part of it, in an inactive state, with lowered (cooler) body temperature.

mammals — animals with hair, that maintain a constant (or fairly constant) body temperature by internal control; the females produce milk to feed their young. They are divided into three sub-groups:
   monotremes that lay eggs;
   marsupials that give birth to young at an early stage of development; their young are then protected in a pouch or pouch area, till they are independent;
   placental mammals that have a well developed placenta (the nutritional connection between the mother and the embryo) so that the embryo can grow in the womb for much longer and to a more advanced stage than in marsupials.

nutritional — providing food.

organism — an individual living thing, plant or animal.

ovum — germ-cell from females; the egg-cell before fertilisation by the sperm.

primitive — early or ancient. Primitive animals are those that evolved earlier; as a result they are usually simpler than animals that evolved later. Nevertheless, they are well suited to living in their environment.

saliva — a fluid made in the lining of the mouth, and released into the mouth to start the process of digesting food; spit.

secrete — in animals, to make special fluids (such as milk and saliva) and release them.

sperm — germ-cell from male animals; has a tail for actively swimming to the ovum.

torpid — in an inactive, sluggish state.

uterus — the womb, that is, the part of the female mammal's reproductive system where the young is nourished and develops.

vagina — tube connecting the womb to the exterior.

yolk — the yellow part of the egg, rich in food to nourish the growing embryo.

INDEX